Wanda
and the Alien

Sue Hendra

For our Wanda

with love from Mummy and Daddy

WANDA AND THE ALIEN A RED FOX BOOK 9781849410182

First published in Great Britain by Red Fox, an imprint of Random House Children's Books A Random House Group Company

This edition published 2011   3 5 7 9 10 8 6 4 2   Copyright © Sue Hendra, 2011

The right of Sue Hendra to be identified as the author of this work has been asserted in accordance with the Copyright, Designs and Patents Act 1988. All rights reserved.

Red Fox Books are published by Random House Children's Books, 61-63 Uxbridge Road, London, W5 5SA www.kidsatrandomhouse.co.uk

Addresses for companies within The Random House Group Limited can be found at: www.randomhouse.co.uk/offices.htm

THE RANDOM HOUSE GROUP Limited Reg. No. 954009

A CIP catalogue record for this book is available from the British Library Printed in Italy

Wanda would never forget the day she met the alien. It was a beautiful summer day and there were flowers everywhere.

She took an instant liking to him

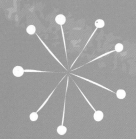

**and held out a paw
in friendship.**

The alien's rocket had crash landed and needed to be mended.

Wanda fetched her tools.

**Wanda and the alien didn't
speak the same language,**

but they made each other laugh a lot.

Soon the rocket was fixed,
but Wanda didn't want the alien
to leave and the alien didn't want to go.

Somehow, together, everything was fun!

Wanda took the alien to meet
her friends at the pond.

But they weren't there.

Where were the ducks,
the frogs and the fish?
It was very strange.

Wanda showed the alien
how to splash instead.

It was fantastic,
so they splashed all day.

Wanda took the alien
up the hill; she wanted him
to meet the squirrels and
all the other rabbits.

But where had they all gone?

Wanda showed the alien
how to roll instead.

They rolled from the top
of the hill to the bottom.

It made them very
dizzy and they loved it.

This was turning out to be the best summer either of them had ever had. But summer can't go on for ever...

Soon autumn comes, the days get shorter, the leaves turn orange and . . .

fall to the ground
leaving the
branches bare!

Only they

weren't bare!

"THERE YOU ARE!" shouted Wanda as she saw all her friends.

"But why have you all been hiding from me?"

"We haven't been hiding from you — we've been hiding from **THE ALIEN!**" they said.

"But this alien is my friend!" said Wanda.

And once they got to know him, the alien was everyone else's friend too.

It wasn't long before they were begging him to stay for Christmas . . .

. . . and Wanda had a funny feeling that this Christmas was going to be the best ever.